MEET SONIC!

A Sonic the Hedgehog Storybook

PENGUIN YOUNG READERS LICENSES
An Imprint of Penguin Random House LLC, New York

Visit us online at www.penguinrandomhouse.com.

ISBN 9780593093931   11

Hey! It's me, Sonic.
As you can probably
tell from looking at me,
I'm a hedgehog.

But I'm no *ordinary* hedgehog.
I like fast things and
exciting adventures.

But that's not the only thing that makes me more than ordinary. I'm also . . .

Faster than the speed of sound!
Some people even call me
the Blue Blur.

Basically, I'm the fastest
living thing in the universe.
Seriously. I am.

But being fast isn't the only thing that matters to me, though it is pretty important.

I also have awesome friends, and they always have my back.

This is Tails. He's my best friend. And he also just so happens to be a fox.

He has two tails that he uses as propellers!

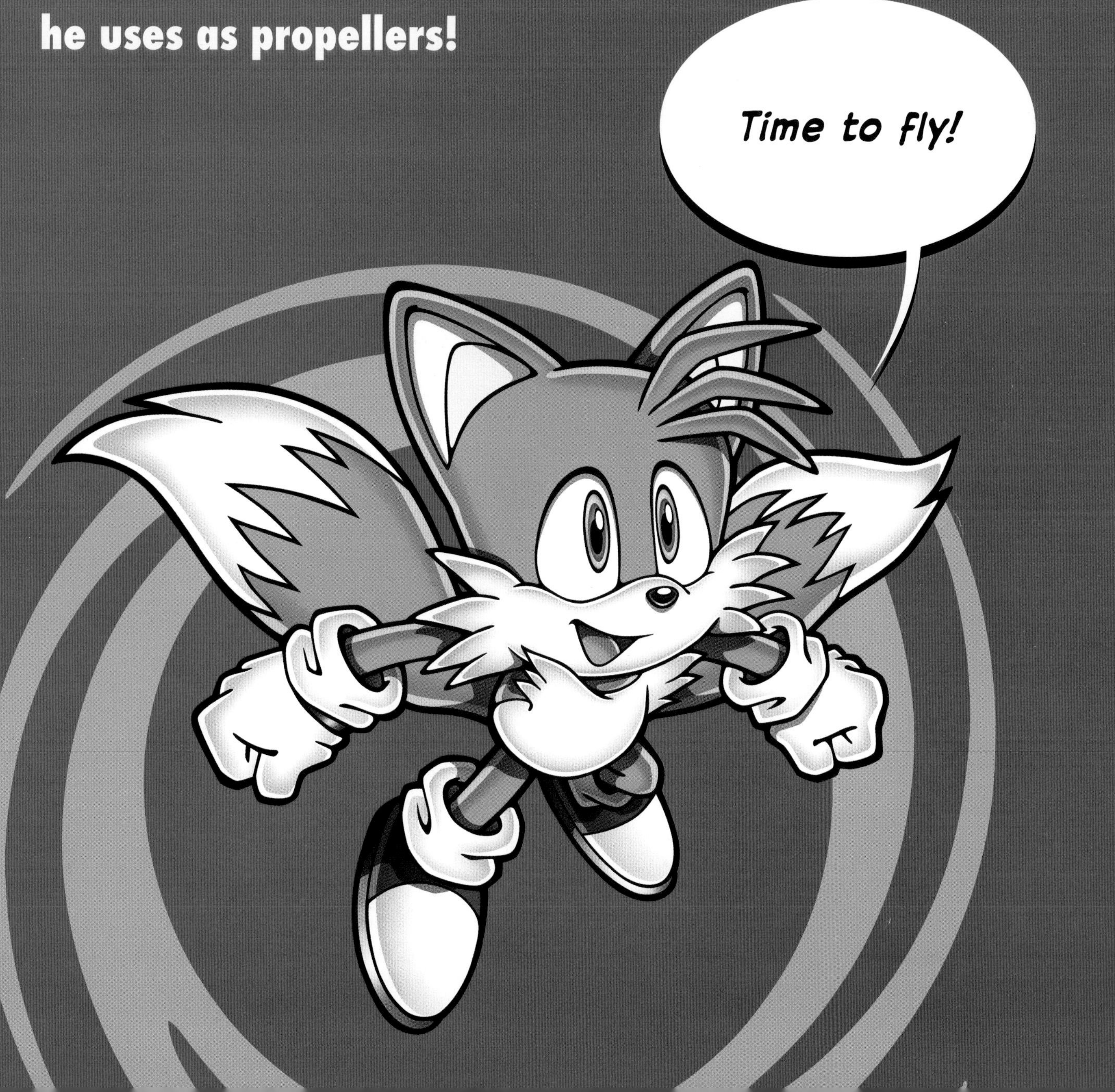

We are always looking for new adventures and we always help each other out. That's what friends are for!

And this is Knuckles. As you might have guessed from his name, he's got huge, spiky knuckles. This tough echidna is one of my closest allies.

He has tons of cool martial-arts skills, and he can punch through walls thanks to his strength, which is *almost* as cool as being super fast.

No time for games!

And last but not least, this friendly pink hedgehog is another one of my closest friends. Her name is Amy, and she's also a tough fighter.

She is super nice, too, probably the sweetest person in our group of friends. But she knows how to bring on the tough when there are bad guys around!

Have no fear!

This is Dr. Eggman,
my evil archenemy. Don't
let his very bushy mustache
fool you. He's super intelligent,
super sinister, and a super villain.
His sole mission is to control the world!

He uses his immense brainpower and scientific know-how to build terrible robotic contraptions and massive machines to carry out his evil plans.

Dr. Eggman is *always* attacking the good people of the world.

I hate that hedgehog!

But no matter how many times he tries to take over the world, my friends and I always work together to send him running!

Still unstoppable!

So just remember: If you stick together, you and your friends will always overcome evil in the end!